# The Story of
# Clan MacWee

### (The smallest clan in Scotland!)

## Alison Mary Fitt & Willie Ritchie

Design - Melvin Creative
Printing – Oriental Press, Dubai

Published by
GW Publishing
PO Box 6091
Thatcham
Berks
RG19 8XZ.

Tel + 44 (0)1635 268080
www.gwpublishing.com

ISBN 978-0-9554145-8-9

# The Story of
# Clan MacWee
## (The smallest clan in Scotland!)

**If Scots words are new to you turn over and look,
you'll find them explained at the back of the book!**

*Publishing*

Many years ago, so the story goes, a strange bunch of people lived in a dark and gloomy Scottish glen. They were known as Clan MacWee, because most of them were no taller than the thistles which grew around their front doors.

The reason they were so small was that for hundreds of years a great muckle black cloud had hung over Glen Wee. So in all that time there hadn't been any sun to make them, or their ancestors, grow. Every morning the Clan Chief, who was called Sma Sandy, shook his fist at it and yelled, "Go away you horrible black cloud."
But of course, it didn't!

They had tried **very** hard to get rid of it! Recently, they had hired the pipe band from Glen Skirl, hoping that the wind from their bag-pipes would **blow** the cloud away.

But although the pipers huffed, puffed and blew until they had no puff left, the cloud hadn't budged.

The MacWees were fed-up. The pipe major made them hand over four sheep, four sacks of flour, and some dosh as well, as payment for the band's services. And they STILL had the cloud to get rid of!

"Now we can fire boulders at that rotten old cloud, and break it up once and for all," they chuckled.

Well, that's what they hoped! But the first boulder they fired soared up in the air…

The second boulder they fired didn't reach the cloud either.
Instead, it walloped down with a muckle THUMP! in the heather,
and woke millions of midgies who had been having their morning nap.

The clansmen who had fired the canon said they were very sorry for the trouble they had caused.

"So you should be," spluttered Sma Sandy, who was slathered in porridge. "I like to EAT my breakfast, not WEAR it! And thanks to you, half the clan are covered in midgie bites!"

He wasn't too mad at them, though. After all, they had only been trying to shift the cloud they all wanted rid of. But it looked as if it was never going to move!

Then one morning, Sma Sandy climbed onto his upturned porridge pot and rallied his clansmen. "Do not lose heart," he told them stoutly. "Let us go into the next glen and see if there is any sun **there** that will make us grow."

You're on, Chief!

They all thought it was a great idea!

At last they reached the top and there, blazing down on them was the sun. The MacWees gaped in amazement. Some had thought the sun was square. Some had argued that it was oblong. And some had even thought it was green with purple stripes! But there it was, up in the sky, big, round, yellow and very warm.

But what the MacWees didn't know was that the glen they were in was called Glen Muckle. And the people who lived there belonged to Clan Muckle. It was called that because for hundreds of years, the sun had shone down there and made everyone grow very tall indeed!

GLEN MUCKLE

Size 20 boots!

But luckily for them, the Muckle clansman had just been to the local Clantucky Fried Chicken shop for his dinner, and he'd gorged himself on so many chickens done in deep batter, he couldn't run very fast at all.

When he finally panted and peched and belched his way into Glen Wee, he couldn't see Clan MacWee anywhere.

Big fat shooglie belly!

GLEN WEE

That's because they were hiding from him!
And do you know what? There and then, the MacWees
decided that being wee wasn't such a bad thing to be after all.
In fact, it was a **brilliant** thing to be, because they could
tuck themselves away in all sorts of nooks and crannies!

# Some words you should know...

| | |
|---|---|
| wee | means small |
| sma | means small too! |
| no' | is what Scots say for not |
| bide | means stay |
| cowp | means fall |
| blaw | means blow |
| fowk | are people |
| daylicht | is daylight |
| jist | means just |
| haud | means hold |
| lugs | means ears (annoying things you have to wash behind) |
| didna | is a Scots version of didn't |

Sma Sandy explains...

| | |
|---|---|
| fitba | that's a football |
| numptie | means idiot (careful who you call that!) |
| muckle | means large |
| stane | is a stone |
| aff | is what Scots might say for off |
| airms | are arms |
| abodie | means everyone |
| cannie | means be careful |
| jine | means join |
| wha | is Scots for who |
| mair | means more |
| drooned | is a Scots word for drowned |
| mak | is make |
| backerties | means backwards |
| braw | means great |
| nyaff | means a small impudent person (don't use this too often either!) |
| rin | means run |
| oot | means out |
| skite | is a Scots word for slip or slide |
| shooglie | means wobbly |